About The Au

The Queen of Crime, the creator of Hercule Poirot and Miss Jane Marple, the best-selling novelist of all time — even people who don't read detective novels know the name Agatha Christie. In her long and prolific career, Christie wrote 66 novels and 14 short story collections, as well as several plays, one of which, *The Mousetrap*, is the longest-running play in history. I've loved Agatha Christie's work ever since I watched my first episode of *Poirot* starring David Suchet (one of the best castings in literary adaptation history), and spent lockdown rereading my favourite Christie mysteries.

The Cornish Mystery

by
Agatha Christie

The Sketch, November 28, 1923

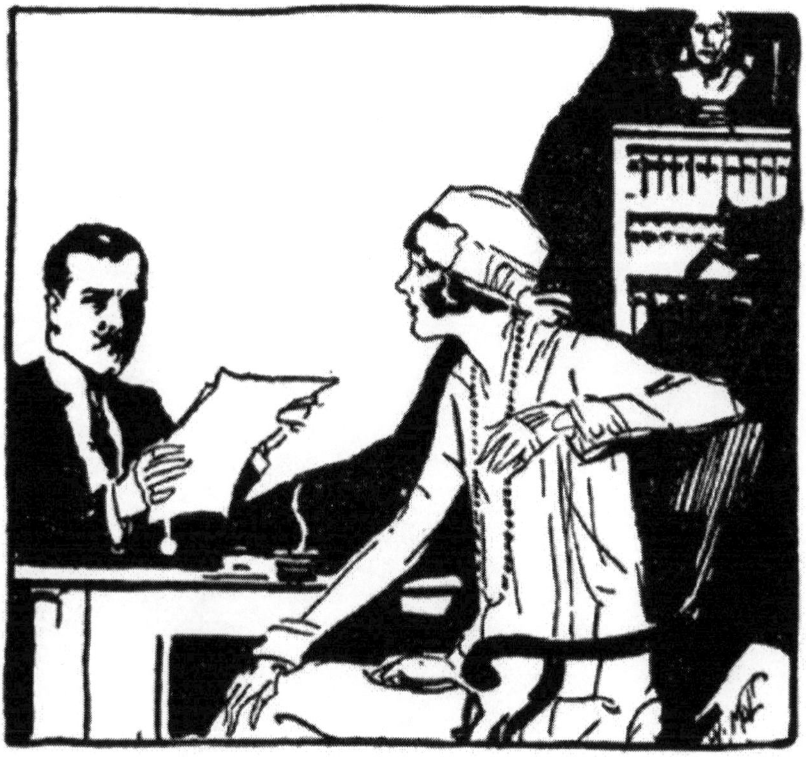

The Cornish Mystery

"Mrs. Pengelley," announced our landlady, and withdrew discreetly.

Many unlikely people came to consult Poirot, but to my mind, the woman who stood nervously just inside the door, fingering her feather neckpiece, was the most unlikely of all. She was so extraordinarily commonplace-a thin, faded woman of about fifty, dressed in a braided coat and skirt, some gold jewellery at her neck, and with her grey hair surmounted by a singularly unbecoming hat. In a country town, you pass a hundred Mrs. Pengelleys in the street every day.

Poirot came forward and greeted her pleasantly, perceiving her obvious embarrassment.

"Madame! Take a chair, I beg of you. My colleague, Captain Hastings."

The lady sat down, murmuring uncertainly: "You are Monsieur Poirot, the detective?"

"At your service, madame."

But our guest was still tongue-tied. She sighed, twisted her fingers, and grew steadily redder and redder.

"There is something I can do for you, eh, madame?"

"Well, I thought-that is-you see-"

"Proceed, madame, I beg of you-proceed."

Mrs. Pengelley, thus encouraged, took a grip on herself.

"It's this way, Monsieur Poirot-I don't want to have anything to do with the police. No, I wouldn't go to the police for anything! But all the same, I'm sorely troubled about something. And yet I don't know if I ought-" She stopped abruptly. "Me, I have nothing to do with the police. My investigations. are strictly private."

Mrs. Pengelley caught at the word.

"Private-that's what I want. I don't want any talk or fuss, or things in the papers. Wicked it is, the way they write things, until the family could never hold up their heads again. And it isn't as though I was even sure it's just a dreadful idea that's come to me, and put it out of my head I can't." She paused for breath. "And all the time I may be wickedly wronging poor. Edward. It's a terrible thought for any wife to have. But you do read of such dreadful things nowadays."

"Permit me-it is of your husband you speak?"

"Yes."

"And you suspect him of-what?"

"I don't like even to say it, Monsieur Poirot. But you do read of such things happening-and the poor souls suspecting nothing."

I was beginning to despair of the lady's ever coming to the point, but Poirot's patience was equal to the demand made upon it.

"Speak without fear, madame. Think what joy will be yours. if we are able to prove your suspicions unfounded."

"That's true-anything's better than this wearing uncertainty. Oh, Monsieur Poirot, I'm dreadfully afraid I'm being poisoned.

"What makes you think so?"

Mrs. Pengelley, her reticence leaving her, plunged into a full recital more suited to the ears of her medical attendant.

"Pain and sickness after food, eh?" said Poirot thoughtfully. "You have a doctor attending you, madame? What does he say?"

"He says it's acute gastritis, Monsieur Poirot. But I can see that he's puzzled and uneasy, and he's always altering the medicine, but nothing does any good."

"You have spoken of your-fears, to him?"

"No, indeed, Monsieur Poirot. It might get about in the town. And perhaps it is gastritis. All the same, it's very odd that whenever Edward is away for the weekend, I'm quite all right again. Even Freda noticed that-my niece, Monsieur Poirot. And then there's that bottle of weed-killer, never used, the gardener says, and yet it's half empty."

She looked appealingly at Poirot. He smiled reassuringly at her, and reached for a pencil and notebook.

"Let us be businesslike, madame. Now, then, you and your husband reside-where?"

"Polgarwith, a small market town in Cornwall."

"You have lived there long?"

"Fourteen years."

"And your household consists of you and your husband. Any children?"

"No."

"But a niece, I think you said?"

"Yes, Freda Stanton, the child of my husband's only sister. She has lived with us for the last eight years-that is, until a week ago."

"Oho, and what happened a week ago?"

"Things hadn't been very pleasant for some time; I don't know what had come over Freda. She was so rude and impertinent, and her temper something shocking, and in the end she flared up one day, and out she walked and took rooms of her own in the town. I've not seen her since. Better leave her to come to her senses, so Mr. Radnor says."

"Who is Mr. Radnor?"

Some of Mrs. Pengelley's initial embarrassment returned. "Oh, he's-he's just a friend. Very pleasant young fellow." "Anything between him and your niece?"

"Nothing whatever," said Mrs. Pengelley emphatically. Poirot shifted his ground.

"You and your husband are, I presume, in comfortable circumstances?"

"Yes, we're very nicely off."

"The money, is it yours or your husband's?"

"Oh, it's all Edward's. I've nothing of my own."

"You see, madame, to be businesslike, we must be brutal. We must seek for a motive. Your husband, he would not poison you just pour passer le temps! Do you know of any reason why he should wish you out of the way?"

"There's the yellow-haired hussy who works for him," said Mrs. Pengelley, with a flash of temper. "My husband's a dentist, Monsieur Poirot, and nothing would do but he must have a smart girl, as he said, with bobbed hair and a white overall, to make his appointments and mix his fillings for him. It's come to my ears that there have been fine goings-on, though of course he swears it's all right."

"This bottle of weed-killer, madame, who ordered it?"
"My husband-about a year ago."

"Your niece, now, has she any money of her own?"

"About fifty pounds a year, I should say. She'd be glad enough to come back and keep house for Edward if I left him."

"You have contemplated leaving him, then?"

"I don't intend to let him have it all his own way. Women aren't the downtrodden slaves they were in old days, Monsieur Poirot."

"I congratulate you on your independent spirit, madame; but let us be practical. You return to Polgarwith today?"

"Yes, I came up by an excursion. Six this morning the train started, and the train goes back at five this afternoon."

"Bien! I have nothing of great moment on hand. I can devote myself to your little affair. Tomorrow I shall be in Polgarwith. Shall we say that Hastings, here, is a distant relative of yours, the son of your second cousin? Me, I am his eccentric foreign friend. In the meantime, eat only what is prepared by your own hands, or under your eye. You have a maid whom you trust?"

"Jessie is a very good girl, I am sure."

"Till tomorrow then, madame, and be of good courage."

Poirot bowed the lady out, and returned thoughtfully to his chair. His absorption was not so great, however, that he failed to see two minute strands of feather scarf wrenched off by the lady's agitated fingers. He collected them carefully and consigned them to the wastepaper basket.

"What do you make of the case, Hastings?"

"A nasty business, I should say.

"Yes, if what the lady suspects be true. But is it? Woe betide any husband who orders a bottle of weed-killer nowadays. If his wife suffers from gastritis, and is inclined to be of a hysterical temperament, the fat is in the fire."

"You think that is all there is to it?"

"Ah-voilà-I do not know, Hastings. But the case interests me-it interests me enormously. For, see you, it has positively no new features. Hence the hysterical theory, and yet Mrs. Pengelley did not strike me as being a hysterical woman. Yes, if I mistake not, we have here a very poignant human drama. Tell me, Hastings, what do you consider Mrs. Pengelley's feelings towards her husband to be?"

"Loyalty struggling with fear," I suggested.

"Yet, ordinarily, a woman will accuse anyone in the world- but not her husband. She will stick to her belief in him through thick and thin."

"The 'other woman' complicates the matter."

"Yes, affection may turn to hate, under the stimulus of jealousy. But hate would take her to the police-not to me. She would want an outcry-a scandal. No, no, let us exercise our little grey cells. Why did she come to me? To have her suspicions proved wrong? Or-to have them proved right? Ah, we have here something I do not understand-an unknown factor. Is she a superb actress, our Mrs. Pengelley? No, she was genuine, I would swear that she was genuine, and therefore I am interested. Look up the trains to Polgarwith, I pray you."

The best train of the day was the one-fifty from Paddington which reached Polgarwith just after seven o'clock. The journey was uneventful, and I had to rouse myself from a pleasant nap to alight upon the platform of the bleak little station. We took our bags to the Duchy Hotel, and after a light meal, Poirot suggested our stepping round to pay an after-dinner call on my so-called cousin.

The Pengelleys' house stood a little way back from the road with an old-fashioned cottage garden in front. The smell of stocks and mignonette came sweetly wafted on the evening breeze. It seemed impossible to associate thoughts of violence with this old-world charm. Poirot rang and knocked. As the summons was not answered, he rang again. This time, after a little pause, the door was opened by a dishevelled-looking servant. Her eyes were red, and she was sniffing violently.

"We wish to see Mrs. Pengelley," explained Poirot. "May we enter?"

The maid stared. Then, with unusual directness, she answered: "Haven't you heard, then? She's dead. Died this evening-about half an hour ago."

We stood staring at her, stunned.

"What did she die of?" I asked at last.

"There's some as could tell." She gave a quick glance over her shoulder. "If it wasn't that somebody ought to be in the house with the missus, I'd pack my box and go tonight. But I'll not leave her dead with no one to watch by her. It's not my place to say anything, and I'm not going to say anything-but everybody knows. It's all over the town. And if Mr. Radnor don't write to the 'Ome Secretary, someone else will. The doctor may say what he likes. Didn't I see the master with my own eyes a-lifting down of the weed-killer from the shelf this very evening? And didn't he jump when he turned round and saw me watching of him? And the missus' gruel there on the table, all ready to take to her? Not another bit of food passes my lips while I am in this house! Not if I dies for it."

"Where does the doctor live who attended your mistress?" "Dr. Adams. Round the corner there in High Street. The second house."

Poirot turned away abruptly. He was very pale.

"For a girl who was not going to say anything, that girl said a lot," I remarked drily.

Poirot struck his clenched hand into his palm.

"An imbecile, a criminal imbecile, that is what I have been, Hastings. I have boasted of my little grey cells, and now I have lost a human life-a life that came to me to be saved. Never did I dream that anything would happen so soon. May the good God forgive me, but I never believed anything would happen at all. Her story seemed to me artificial. Here we are at the doctor's. Let us see what he can tell us."

Dr. Adams was the typical genial red-faced country doctor of fiction. He received us politely enough, but at a hint of our errand, his red face became purple.

"Damned nonsense! Damned nonsense, every word of it! Wasn't I in attendance on the case? Gastritis-gastritis pure and simple. This town's a hotbed of gossip-a lot of scandal- mongering old women get together and invent God knows. what. They read these scurrilous rags of newspapers, and nothing will suit them but that someone in their town shall get poisoned too. They see a bottle of weed-killer on a shelf-and hey presto!-away goes their imagination with the bit between its teeth. I know Edward Pengelley-he wouldn't poison his grandmother's dog. And why should he poison his wife? Tell me that?"

"There is one thing, Monsieur le Docteur, that perhaps you do not know."

And, very briefly, Poirot outlined the main facts of Mrs. Pengelley's visit to him. No one could have been more astonished than Dr. Adams. His eyes almost started out of his head.

"God bless my soul!" he ejaculated. "The poor woman must have been mad. Why didn't she speak to me? That was the proper thing to do."

"And have her fears ridiculed?"

"Not at all, not at all. I hope I've got an open mind."

Poirot looked at him and smiled. The physician was evidently more perturbed than he cared to admit. As we left the house, Poirot broke into a laugh.

"He is as obstinate as a pig, that one. He has said it is gastritis; therefore it is gastritis! All the same, he has the mind uneasy."

"What's our next step?"

"A return to the inn, and a night of horror upon one of your English provincial beds, mon ami. It is a thing to make pity, the cheap English bed!"

"And tomorrow?"

"Rien à faire. We must return to town and await developments.

"That's very tame," I said, disappointed. "Suppose there are none?"

"There will be! I can promise you that. Our old doctor may give as many certificates as he pleases. He cannot stop several hundred tongues from wagging. And they will wag to some purpose, I can tell you that!"

Our train for town left at eleven the following morning. Before we started for the station, Poirot expressed a wish to see Miss Freda Stanton, the niece mentioned to us by the dead woman. We found the house where she was lodging easily enough. With her was a tall, dark young man whom she introduced in some confusion as Mr. Jacob Radnor. Miss Freda Stanton was an extremely pretty girl of the old Cornish type-dark hair and eyes and rosy cheeks. There was a flash in those same dark eyes which told of a temper that it would not be wise to provoke.

"Poor Auntie," she said, when Poirot had introduced himself and explained his business. "It's terribly sad. I've been wishing all the morning that I'd been kinder and more patient."

"You stood a great deal, Freda," interrupted Radnor.

"Yes, Jacob, but I've got a sharp temper, I know. After all, it was only silliness on Auntie's part. I ought to have just laughed and not minded. Of course, it's all nonsense her thinking that Uncle was poisoning her. She was worse after any food he gave her-but I'm sure it was only from thinking about it. She made up her mind she would be, and then she was."

"What was the actual cause of your disagreement, mademoiselle?"

Miss Stanton hesitated, looking at Radnor. That young gentleman was quick to take the hint.

"I must be getting along, Freda. See you this evening. Good-bye, gentlemen; you're on your way to the station, I suppose?"

Poirot replied that we were, and Radnor departed.

"You are affianced, is it not so?" demanded Poirot, with a sly smile.

Freda Stanton blushed and admitted that such was the case.

"And that was really the whole trouble with Auntie," she added.

"She did not approve of the match for you?"

"Oh, it wasn't that so much. But you see, she-"The girl came to a stop.

"Yes?" encouraged Poirot gently.

"It seems rather a horrid thing to say about her-now she's dead. But you'll never understand unless I tell you. Auntie was absolutely infatuated with Jacob."

"Indeed?"

"Yes, wasn't it absurd? She was over fifty, and he's not quite thirty! But there it was. She was silly about him! I had to tell her at last that it was me he was after-and she carried on dreadfully. She wouldn't believe a word of it, and was so rude and insulting that it's no wonder I lost my temper. I talked it over with Jacob, and we agreed that the best thing to do was for me to clear out for a bit till she came to her senses. Poor Auntie- I suppose she was in a queer state altogether."

"It would certainly seem so. Thank you, mademoiselle, for making things so clear to me.

A little to my surprise, Radnor was waiting for us in the street below.

"I can guess pretty well what Freda has been telling you," he remarked. "It was a most unfortunate thing to happen, and very awkward for me, as you can imagine. I need hardly say that it was none of my doing. I was pleased at first, because I imagined the old woman was helping on things with Freda. The whole thing was absurd-but extremely unpleasant."

"When are you and Miss Stanton going to be married?" "Soon, I hope. Now, Monsieur Poirot, I'm going to be candid with you. I know a bit more than Freda does. She believes her uncle to be innocent. I'm not so sure. But I can tell you one thing: I'm going to keep my mouth shut about what I do know. Let sleeping dogs lie. I don't want my wife's uncle tried and hanged for murder."

"Why do you tell me all this?"

"Because I've heard of you, and I know you're a clever man.

It's quite possible that you might ferret out a case against him But I put it to you-what good is that? The poor woman is past help, and she'd have been the last person to want a scandal-why, she'd turn in her grave at the mere thought of it."

"You are probably right there. You want me to-hush it up, then?"

That's my idea. I'll admit frankly that I'm selfish about it. I've got my way to make-and I'm building up a good little business as a tailor and outfitter.

"Most of us are selfish, Mr. Radnor. Not all of us admit it so freely. I will do what you ask-but I tell you frankly you will not succeed in hushing it up."

"Why not?"

Poirot held up a finger. It was market day, and we were passing the market a busy hum came from within.

"The voice of the people that is why, Mr. Radnor. Ah, we must run, or we shall miss our train.

"Very interesting, is it not, Hastings?" said Poirot, as the train steamed out of the station.

He had taken out a small comb from his pocket, also a microscopic mirror, and was carefully arranging his moustache, the symmetry of which had become slightly impaired during our brisk run.

21

"You seem to find it so," I replied. "To me, it is all rather sordid and unpleasant. There's hardly any mystery about it.".

"I agree with you; there is no mystery whatever."

"I suppose we can accept the girl's rather extraordinary story of her aunt's infatuation? That seemed the only fishy part to me She was such a nice, respectable woman.

"There is nothing extraordinary about that—it is completely ordinary. If you read the papers carefully, you will find that often a nice respectable woman of that age leaves a husband she has lived with for twenty years, and sometimes a whole family of children as well, in order to link her life with that of a young man considerably her junior. You admire les femmes, Hastings; you prostrate yourself before all of them who are good-looking and have the good taste to smile upon you; but psychologically you know nothing whatever about them. In the autumn of at woman's life, there comes always one mad moment when she longs for romance, for adventure-before it is too late. It comes none the less surely to a woman because she is the wife of a respectable dentist in a country town!"

"And you think-"

"That a clever man might take advantage of such a moment. "I shouldn't call Pengelley so clever," I mused. "He's got the whole town by the ears. And yet I suppose you're right. The only two men who know anything, Radnor and the doctor, both want to hush it up. He's managed that somehow. I wish we'd seen the fellow.'

"You can indulge your wish. Return by the next train and invent an aching molar.

I looked at him keenly.

"I wish I knew what you considered so interesting about the

"My interest is very aptly summed up by a remark of yours, Hastings. After interviewing the maid, you observed that for someone who was not going to say a word, she had said a good deal.

"Oh!" I said doubtfully, then I harped back to my original criticism: "I wonder why you made no attempt to see Pengelley?"

"Mon ami, I give him just three months. Then I shall see him for as long as I please in the dock."

For once I thought Poirot's prognostications were going to be proved wrong. The time went by, and nothing transpired as to our Cornish case. Other matters occupied us, and I had nearly forgotten the Pengelley tragedy when it was suddenly recalled to me by a short paragraph in the paper which stated that an order to exhume the body of Mrs. Pengelley had been obtained from the Home Secretary.

A few days later, and "The Cornish Mystery" was the topic of every paper. It seemed that gossip had never entirely died down, and when the engagement of the widower to Miss Marks, his secretary, was announced, the tongues burst out again louder than ever. Finally a petition was sent to the Home Secretary; the body was exhumed, large quantities of arsenic were discovered; and Mr. Pengelley was arrested and charged with the murder of his wife.

Poirot and I attended the preliminary proceedings. The evidence was much as might have been expected. Dr. Adams admitted that the symptoms of arsenical poisoning might easily be mistaken for those of gastritis. The Home Office expert gave his evidence; the maid Jessie poured out a flood of voluble information, most of which was rejected, but which certainly strengthened the case against the prisoner. Freda Stanton gave evidence as to her aunt's being worse whenever she ate food prepared by her husband. Jacob Radnor told how he had dropped in unexpectedly on the day of Mrs. Pengelley's death, and found Pengelley replacing the bottle of weed-killer on the pantry shelf, Mrs. Pengelley's gruel being on the table close by. Then Miss Marks, the fair-haired secretary, was called, and wept and went into hysterics and admitted that there had been passages" between her and her employer, and that he had promised to marry her in the event of anything happening to his wife. Pengelley reserved his defence and was sent for trial. Jacob Radnor walked back with us to our lodgings,

"You see, Monsieur Radnor," said Poirot, "I was right. The voice of the people spoke-and with no uncertain voice. There was to be no hushing up of this case.

"You were quite right," sighed Radnor. "Do you see any chance of his getting off?"

"Well, he has reserved his defence. He may have something up the sleeve, as you English say. Come in with us, will you not?"

Radnor accepted the invitation. I ordered two whiskies and sodas and a cup of chocolate. The last order caused consternat tion, and I much doubted whether it would ever put in an appearance.

"Of course," continued Poirot, "I have a good deal of experience in matters of this kind. And I see only one loophole of escape for our friend."

"What is it?".

"That you should sign this paper."

With the suddenness of a conjurer, he produced a sheet of paper covered with writing.

"What is it?"

"A confession that you murdered Mrs. Pengelley." There was a moment's pause; then Radnor laughed. "You must be mad!"

"No, no, my friend, I am not mad. You came here; you started a little business; you were short of money. Mr.

25

Pengelley was a man very well-to-do. You met his niece; she was inclined to smile upon you. But the small allowance that Pengelley might have given her upon her marriage was not enough for you. You must get rid of both the uncle and the aunt, then the money would come to her, since she was the only relative. How elev.erly you set about it! You made love to that plain middle-aged woman until she was your slave. You implanted in her doubts of her husband. She discovered first that he was deceiving her then, under your guidance, that he was trying to poison her. You were often at the house; you had opportunities to introduce the arsenic into her food. But you were careful never to do so when her husband was away. Being a woman, she did not keep her suspicions to herself. She talked to her niece; doubtless she talked to other women friends. Your only difficulty was keeping up separate relations with the two women, and even that was not so difficult as it looked. You explained to the aunt that, to allay the suspicions of her husband, you had to pretend to pay court to the niece. And the younger lady needed little convinc ing — she would never seriously consider her aunt as a rival.

"But then Mrs. Pengelley made up her mind, without saying anything to you, to consult me. If she could be really assured, beyond any possible doubt, that her husband was trying to poison her, she would feel justified in leaving him, and linking her life with yours- which is what she imagined you wanted her to do. But that did not suit your book at all. You did not want a detective prying around. A favourable minute occurs. You are in the house when Mr. Pengelley is getting some gruel for his wife, and you introduce the fatal dose. The rest is easy. Apparently anxious to hush matters up, you secretly foment them. But you reckoned without Hercule Poirot, my intelligent young friend. Radnor was deadly pale, but he still endeavoured to carry off matters with a high hand.

"Very interesting and ingenious, but why tell me all this?" "Because, monsieur, I represent-not the law, but Mrs. Pengelley. For her sake, I give you a chance of escape Sign this paper, and you shall have twenty-four hours start-twenty-four hours before I place it in the hands of the police."

Radnor hesitated.

"You can't prove anything."

"Can't I? I am Hercule Poirot. Look out of the window, monsieur. There are two men in the street. They have orders not to lose sight of you."

Radnor strode across to the window and pulled aside the blind, then shrank back with an oath. "You see, monsieur? Sign-it is your best chance."

"What guarantee have I-"

"That I shall keep faith? The word of Hercule Poirot. You will sign? Good. Hastings, be so kind as to pull that left-hand blind halfway up. That is the signal that Mr. Radnor may leave unmolested."

White, muttering oaths, Radnor hurried from the room. Poirot nodded gently.

"A coward! I always knew it'

"It seems to me, Poirot, that you've acted in a criminal manner," I cried angrily. "You always preach against sentiment. And here you are letting a dangerous criminal escape out of sheer sentimentality.

"That was not sentiment-that was business," replied Poirot. "Do you not see, my friend, that we have no shadow of proof against him? Shall I get up and say to twelve stolid Cornishmen that I Hercule Poirot, know? They would laugh at me. The only chance was to frighten him and get a confession that way. Those two loafers that I noticed outside came in very useful. Pull down the blind again, will you, Hastings? Not that there was any reason for raising it. It was part of the mise en scène.

"Well, well, we must keep our word. Twenty-four hours, did I say? So much longer for poor Mr. Pengelley-and it is not more than he deserves; for mark you, he deceived his wife. I am very strong on the family life, as you know. Ah, well, twenty-four hours and then? I have great faith in Scotland Yard. They will get him, mon ami they will get him.

THE END

Made in the USA
Monee, IL
14 July 2024